Party Fun with Kant

The German List

Nicolas Mahler

PARTY FUN WITH KANT

-Philosofunnies-

Translated by James Reidel

Seagull
BOOKS

LONDON NEW YORK CALCUTTA

This publication was supported by a grant from
the Goethe-Institut, India

Seagull Books, 2018

First published in English by Seagull Books, 2018
English translation © James Reidel, 2018

ISBN 978 0 8574 2 536 2

British Library Cataloguing-in-Publication Data
A catalogue record for this book is available from the British Library

Typeset by Seagull Books, Calcutta, India
Printed and bound by Hyam Enterprises, Calcutta, India

PARTY FUN
WITH KANT

'Then I thought of Plato's words
and felt them in my heart:
"Everything that is human doesn't
merit this enormous seriousness;
nevertheless—"'

FRIEDRICH NIETZSCHE,
Human, All Too Human

PLATO'S
TESTIMONY

This one was, so to speak,
male-female.

Furthermore, the entire figure was round, such that the backsides and the chest formed into a circle.

And each one had four arms and as many legs as arms . . .

... and two faces on a cylindrical neck, one perfectly like the other ...

... and a common head for both faces facing away from each other ...

RHINOPLASTY
À LA ARISTOTLE

Emerging things emerge in part from nature, in part through artifice and, in part, in a spontaneous manner.

In regard to these things, there exists a problem.

Namely, when a snub nose and concave nose are identical, such that the snubness and the concavity are identical.

But when this is not the case, then it
is either impossible to speak of a
snub nose . . .

. . . or the same will be said
twice: a concave nose nose,

For the snub nose will be a concave nose nose.

Hence, it would be absurd if such a thing were to become a what-does-this-mean-to-be.

But if not, then there would exist never-ending regression.

For in a snub nose nose, something else will still be involved.

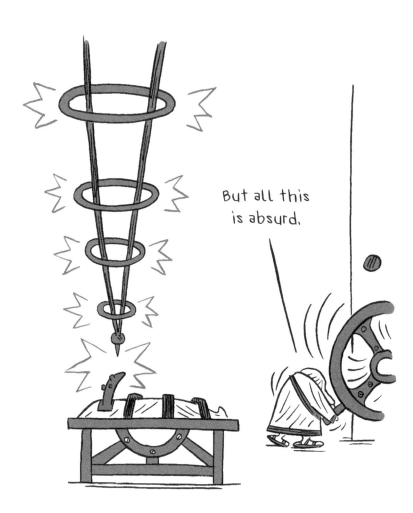

But all this
is absurd.

EPICURUS' SEX EDUCATION

As I understand you, your restless flesh drives you in an especially intense way to the pleasure of love,

Follow your urge as you want, but don't overstep the law . . .

. . . don't violate public morals . . .

24

...nor waste the things
you need to live.

But it's impossible not to be
ensnared by at least one of
these unpleasantries...

DO NOTHING IN YOUR LIFE
WHICH WILL INSTIL FEAR
WHEN YOUR NEIGHBOURS
KNOW ABOUT IT!

COFFEE KLATCH WITH HILDEGARD VON BINGEN

There are men who have
thick, white and dry brains.

They show themselves to be bold in their demeanour, but in their works this boldness isn't found . . .

The wind in their loins has only a rather tepid fire, such that it only warms a little, like water that is barely warm.

Brrrr.

And the two tabernacles, which ought
to stir the fire like bellows, are not
strong enough

...for in them there is not
the fullness of the fire,

They have true love for no one,
they are always embittered,
covetous and brutal,

If such men have to couple with women,
they then wither away inside and come
along like one dying . . .

... when they cannot, in the extremes of dreams, thoughts or in some other unnatural thing, emit the spuma of their seed.

Oh, stop it Hilde!

MEISTER ECKHART'S STREET SERMON

.

the angel sweareth upon his
eternal life that time would
never more be,

Our Lord speaketh to
his disciples:

A thing small and few and short, and ye shall seeth me not.

St Bernard speaketh: That the eye is liketh heaven; it receiveth heaven in itself.

42

Methinketh that this word
hath four meanings...

Now mark thee! One
meaning is...

M. DE MONTAIGNE, EDITOR-IN-CHIEF

I see that the best of
the ancient poets avoided
all this effort, all this
ornamentation.

Seneca is full of sharp sallies and witty conceits.

Plutarch full of things.

Those masters of the art have no need of all this holding the hand up to make us understand. They find laughter everywhere and they don't need to tickle themselves first.

To boldly and bravely tell the truth, _his_ kind of writing bores me, just like everything about him.

His prefatory remarks, his definitions, his etymologies detract from the greatest part of his work.

What still remains therein of the pit and marrow is held together by boring decorations.

I already know enough about what death and lust is without frittering away my time as someone anatomically dismembers me.

The following passage caught my eye: Ego vero me minus diu senem esse mallem, quam esse senem, atequam essem.

These words are lost on me.

ADVENTURES IN THE UNIVERSE WITH 'MODESTY' BLAISE PASCAL

...I am terribly ignorant in everything.

I see that appalling vastness of the cosmos that encloses me...

...and I find myself restricted to a corner of this enormous space...

...without knowing why I am put in this place and not in another instead...

... and this brief duration, which has been provided for my existence, at this exact point in time ...

... and not to some other instead in all the eternity that came before me and in all the eternity that comes after me ...

Distractions are the only thing that consoles us in our misery.

SOCIETY REPORTER JEAN-JACQUES ROUSSEAU

Man is born free, and finds
himself everywhere in chains.

Who believes himself to be a
master over others is more a
slave than they.

How did you come
to this way of
life?

All power comes from God, that I admit;
however, every disease comes from Him.
Does this mean that it is forbidden to
call a doctor?

How is it that freedom will only be maintained with the help of servitude?

'Voting by lot,' writes Montesquieu, 'is the nature of democracy.'

I agree with that . . .

And now, statisticians, over to you; the matter is in your hands: Count, measure, compare!

PARTY FUN
WITH KANT

What about
satisfaction during
the course of life?

Passions are a cancer for a purely
practical reason and are incurable
for the most part.

The concepts of reality, substance,
causality, even that of necessity in
existence, have no relevance.

To sleep long is a savings on adversity!

A few years ago, I would be afflicted by a cough and runny nose every now and then,

Tobacco—whether smoked or
taken as snuff—is associated with
an unpleasant sensation.

Diapering among the barbarous races
doesn't take place at all.

The bed is the nest for a
host of diseases.

Eating alone for a
philosophizing scholar is
unhealthy.

LICHTENBERG'S
WEEKLY PLANNER

MONDAY

Ideas for work and chitchat.

TUESDAY

Calculate how much younger one
would be if one rises at three o'clock
in the morning.

WEDNESDAY

He gave names to a pair
of slippers.

THURSDAY

Perhaps our earth is
female.

FRIDAY

Admittedly, this seems
otherwise to the bearded.

SATURDAY

He stood so sad there, like
the little feeding dish for
a dead bird.

SUNDAY

A revelation is
missing here.

AT AN ART EXHIBITION WITH HEGEL

This art exhibition includes
several paintings that have
subjects borrowed from poetry.

If one looks at these paintings more often
and in greater detail, before long, they will
appear saccharine and insipid.

Then one wonders what could be the
interest, the intention of someone who
produces such content and presents it in the
form of a work of art.

This reveals to us
something trivial.

This is thoroughly
barbaric.

Just as the Prophet said, according to the *Sunna*, to the two women, Ommi Habiba and Ommi Selma, who told him about the icons in Ethiopian churches:

These images will condemn their creators on the Day of Judgement.

To provide some contrast, we have equally fine genre paintings at our art exhibition this year.

We see, for example, a wife, who is entering an inn, so as to scold her husband.

Genre paintings of this variety now,
however, must be small. It would
be intolerable to see such works
rendered life-size.

SCHOPENHAUER'S DRIVING SCHOOL

There exists in the world only
<u>one</u> lying creature: it is <u>man</u>.

'Everything for me, and
nothing for anyone else'—
is his watchword.

These so-called human beings are
nearly always nothing but watery gruel
with some arsenic.

What makes human beings hard-hearted
is this: each one of them bears enough
problems of his own or thinks he does,

Human beings require occupations on
the outside for they have nothing on
the inside,

By far most human beings
are inaccessible to purely
intellectual pleasures.

Matrimony is not the setting for witty
conversation but, rather, to achieve the
begetting of children.

For many people, philosophers are
tiresome night owls who annoy
them during sleep.

Being stupid and being vile is not against
the law: *ineptire est juris gentium.*
However, to talk of stupidity and
vileness is a crime.

In the end, one is only really honest with himself and at most with his children.

DR KIERKEGAARD'S
PRACTICE

Fear is a force in motion
through which sorrow bores
into our heart.

All earthly existence is a
kind of sickness,

Every person is only a tool that
doesn't know when the moment
comes when it is put aside,

Oh! Death! Great is
your Persuasion,

No one comes back from the dead, no one comes into the world without tears.

No one asks if one wants in, no one asks if one wants out.

What is more disconsolate than
when the wanderer must say:
There is no longer a way here.

Hang yourself, you
will regret it.

AT THE SUPERMARKET
WITH KARL MARX

Conscious vital activity intuitively
distinguishes humans from the vital
activity of animals.

Estranged labour reverses this relationship such that man makes his vital activity, his _being_, a means to his existence.

We now take it further, how this notion of estranged, externalized labour must be expressed and represented in reality.

CAMP
FRIEDRICH
NIETZSCHE

We so love being outdoors
in Nature, for it has no
opinions in regard to us!

And so forward on the path of wisdom,
bold steps, bold faith!

Strong waters take away many a
stone and bush, strong minds
many stupid and addled
brains.

The public easily mistakes him who fishes in troubled waters with him who draws from the depths.

All good things have something apathetic about them and lie like cows in a meadow.

How can man take
pleasure in nonsense?

The plots, which Wagner knew how
to effectively unravel with the help
of dramatic effects, are quite
another matter.

Fire and ash, shall he groan and
bellow at me:
THAT IS HOW I LIKE BEASTS TO
ANSWER ME!

Listen to the second act of
Twilight of the Gods without
the drama: it is chaotic music,
as wild as a bad dream.

In solitude the solitary man eats himself up, in the multitude, they eat him up.

Now choose.

BEDTIME STORIES WITH BERTRAND RUSSELL

Nor have the lives of important men
been thrilling affairs save a few
great moments.

All the contemporary abundance of boredom
should be borne in mind when thinking of
the world of a hundred years ago . . .

. . . and when one goes further back,
it gets even worse.

Surely boredom was in great part what led to witch-burnings, which made for the sole sport that could enliven winter evenings.

Wars, pogroms and persecutions can all be ascribed to the flight from boredom.

Even children should be taught this
faculty to endure a more or less
monotonous life.

WITTGENSTEIN'S BROOM SKETCH

You want the broom?
And why do you put it
so strangely?

Well, if the broom is located there,
that means the handle and brush must
be there, and in a certain position to
one another.

Yes, the broom will be disassembled if
you take the stick and the brush apart;
but then the instruction is to bring the
broom from its constituent parts?

But you will not deny that a specific instruction in (a) says the same thing as one in (b).

Yes and no.

HA HA HA HA HA HA

A DREAM WEDDING WITH SIMONE DE BEAUVOIR

Surely there also exists a morbid contrast between the pomp of a big funeral and the putrefaction of the grave,

But a dead man does not wake up when he is carried to the grave,

Obviously, the expression 'a hole is a hole' is a crude joke.

More than a few men are
rendered impotent on the
wedding night simply due to
the marriage ceremony.

E. M. CIORAN, FORTUNE COOKIE WRITER

A monster haunts us.

If one were but born before humanity.

It is better to be an insect than a human being, a plant than an insect,

and so on.

We should have been spared dragging around a body. The burden of the EGO is sufficient.

We have not yet digested the humiliation of being born.

The amount of fatigue that rests in my brain.

My vision of the future is so definite that if I were to have children, I would immediately strangle them.

Whether or not one kills himself, everything remains unchanged.

If one thinks about it, so many and many more have managed to die!

BARTHES
THE BEAR

I have encountered millions of bodies in my life.

Of these millions I could only
desire a few hundred.

That is
my type!

That is not my type at
all.

That is very much
my type.

Speaking of pickups: Is the lover only a sophisticated 'pickup artist', who seeks for 'his type' all of his life?

What part of my Other's body provides me with a reading of my truth?

A tough
nut.

This being,
whom I await, is
not a real one.

DELEUZE
LEAVES THE
CINEMA

Nothing but clichés,
clichés everywhere . . .

A swarm of characters, between whom there are only weak points of contact and who are the main characters and then return to being minor characters.

Events that are imposed on them but which don't concern them, those who provoke them or those who are subject to them.

All of this gets cemented by the
established clichés of an epoch
or of a moment.

The physical—visual and auditory—and
psychic clichés feed off each other.

For people endure themselves and the world, misery has to have penetrated their inner consciousness...

...and the interior must match the exterior.

Both the action-image and the American dream are affected by this crisis.

In the Western, this problem arises under especially fertile conditions.

TO THE GALLOWS, BASTARDO!

MICHEL FOUCAULT'S CABINET OF CURIOSITIES

I would like to present for you today
a mixed figure: a monster, a childish
onanist and a shrewish woman.

CHARLES JOUY, the simpleton, the village idiot!

HENRIETTE CORNIER, this is an utter landscape on its own ... this maidservant who, without the least discursive expenditure, decapitated a baby girl!

The third is the 'MASTURBATOR'!
Masturbation is a universal
secret, but one that no one
shares with others.

and lastly, the most unassuming,
the most discreet and the least
scientifically charged figure:
THE WOMAN OF SÉLESTAT!

This character is superimposed on the other characters and finally coalesces all the essential problems that circle around the anomaly!

We ought to discuss what I have presented.
Sometimes very little would be enough to
straighten everything out—a question.

But this question
never comes up.

My relationship to the people
in attendance is like that of
an actor or an acrobat.

And when I stop speaking,
the sensation is of total
isolation.

SOURCES

This is a work of satire that relies on the following sources from the German. Mahler employs the philosophers' own words as well as their work in German translation to achieve his sight gags and contextual humour. Even the detail in the sources is both the adherence to and send-up of scholarly erudition. In keeping with Mahler's convention, I have chosen to be faithful to these sources rather than their English counterparts. [Trans.]

PLATO'S TESTIMONY

Pages 7–11 Plato, 'Symposion' [Symposium] in *Sämtliche Werke* [Collected Works] VOL. 4 (Karlheinz Hülser ed. and Friedrich Schleiermacher and Franz Susemihl trans). Frankfurt am Main: Insel Verlag, 1991, 189–90d.

RHINOPLASTY À LA ARISTOTLE

Page 15 Aristotle, *Metaphysik: Bücher 7 und 8* [Metaphysics: Books 7 and 8] (Wolfgang Detel and Jula Wildberger trans). Frankfurt am Main: Suhrkamp Verlag, 2009, p. 39.

Pages 16–19 Aristotle, *Metaphysik*, p. 31.

Page 20 Aristotle, *Metaphysik*, p. 91.

EPICURUS' SEX EDUCATION

Pages 23–8 Epicurus, *Philosophie der Freude: Briefe, Hauptlehrsätze, Spruchsammlung, Fragmente* [Philosophy of Pleasure: Letters, Principal Doctrines, Sayings, Fragments] (Paul M. Laskowsky trans.). Frankfurt am Main: Insel Verlag, 1988, pp. 84 and 88.

COFFEE KLATCH WITH HILDEGARD VON BINGEN

Pages 31–3 Hildegard von Bingen, 'Von den Phlegmatikern' [On Phlegmatic Men] in *Wisse die Wege: Ratschläge fürs Leben* [Know the Way: Advice for Living] (Johannes Bühler ed. and trans.). Frankfurt am Main: Insel Verlag, 2008, p. 87.

Page 34 ABOVE Hildegard von Bingen, 'Von den Melancholikern' [On Melancholy Men] in *Wisse die Wege*, p. 86.

Page 34 BELOW Hildegard von Bingen, 'Von der Verbannung des Adam' [On the Banishment of Adam] in *Wisse die Wege*, p. 83ff.

Page 35 ABOVE Hildegard von Bingen, 'Von der Verbannung des Adam', p. 84.

Page 36 Hildegard von Bingen, 'Vierte Vision' [Fourth Vision] in *Wisse die Wege*, p. 281.

MEISTER ECKHART'S STREET SERMON

Page 39 Meister Eckhart, 'Sermon 70' in *Werke 2: Texte und Übersetzungen* [Works 2: Texts and Translations] (Ernst Benz, Karl Christ, Bruno Decker, Heribert Fischer, Bernhard Geyer, Josef Koch, Josef Quint, Konrad Weiss and Albert Zimmermann trans and Niklaus Largier ed.). Frankfurt am Main: Deutscher Klassiker Verlag, 2008, p. 58.

Page 40 ABOVE Eckhart, 'Sermon 70', p. 58.

Page 40 BELOW Eckhart, 'Sermon 70', p. 56.

Page 41 ABOVE Eckhart, 'Sermon 70', p. 56.

Page 41 BELOW Eckhart, 'Sermon 70', p. 58.

Page 42 ABOVE Eckhart, 'Sermon 75' and 'Sermon 72', pp. 116 and 84.

Page 42 BELOW Eckhart, 'Sermon 72', p. 84.

Page 43 ABOVE Eckhart, 'Sermon 71', p. 64

Page 43 BELOW Eckhart, 'Sermon 71' and 'Sermon 66', pp. 64 and 11.

M. DE MONTAIGNE, EDITOR-IN-CHIEF

Page 47 Michel de Montaigne, 'Über Bücher' [On Books] in *Essais* (Johann Joachim Bode trans.). Frankfurt am Main: Insel Verlag, 2001, p.119.

Page 48 ABOVE Montaigne, 'Über Bücher', p. 122.

Page 48 BELOW Montaigne, 'Über Bücher', p. 119ff.

Pages 49–50 Montaigne, 'Über Bücher', p. 122.

Page 51 ABOVE Montaigne, 'Über Bücher', p. 126. [*Ego vero me minus diu senem esse mallem* . . . From Cicero's *De Senectute* (*On Old Age*), literally, 'But I had rather not be an old man, so long as I might be, than be old before I should be.']

Page 51 BELOW 'Über Bücher', p. 123.

ADVENTURES IN THE UNIVERSE WITH 'MODESTY' BLAISE PASCAL

Page 53 The title alludes to the 1960s British comic-strip character Modesty Blaise. [Trans.]

Page 55 Blaise Pascal, 'Zwischen Größe und Elend' [Between Greatness and Misery] in *Gedanken* [Thoughts] (Ulrich Kunzmann trans.). Berlin: Suhrkamp Verlag, 2012, p. 43.

Page 56 ABOVE Pascal, 'Zwischen Größe und Elend', p. 43.

Page 56 BELOW Pascal, 'Zwischen Größe und Elend', p. 44.

Pages 57–9 Pascal, 'Zwischen Größe und Elend', p. 44.

Page 60 Pascal, 'Zerstreuungen' [Distractions] in *Gedanken*, p. 82.

SOCIETY REPORTER JEAN-JACQUES ROUSSEAU

Pages 63–4 Jean-Jacques Rousseau, *Vom Gesellschaftsvertrag oder Grundlagen des politischen Rechts* [The Social Contract or the Principles of Political Rights] (Erich Wolfgang Skwara trans.). Frankfurt am Main: Insel Verlag, 1996, p. 10.

Page 65 ABOVE Rousseau, *Vom Gesellschaftsvertrag*, p. 10.

Page 65 BELOW Rousseau, *Vom Gesellschaftsvertrag*, p. 15.

Page 66 ABOVE Rousseau, *Vom Gesellschaftsvertrag*, p. 129.

Page 66 BELOW Rousseau, *Vom Gesellschaftsvertrag*, p. 144.

Page 67 ABOVE Rousseau, *Vom Gesellschaftsvertrag*, p. 144.

Page 67 BELOW Rousseau, *Vom Gesellschaftsvertrag*, p. 182

Page 68 Rousseau, *Vom Gesellschaftsvertrag*, p. 115.

PARTY FUN WITH KANT

Page 71 Immanuel Kant, 'Von der langen Weile und dem Kurzweil' [On Boredom and Amusement] in *Werke*, VOL. 6 (Wilhelm Weischedel ed.). Frankfurt am Main: Insel Verlag, 1964, p. 556.

Page 72 ABOVE Kant, 'Von den Leidenschaften' [On the Passions] in *Werke*, VOL. 6, p. 600.

Page 72 BELOW Immanuel Kant, 'Von der Endabsicht der natürlichen Dialektik der menschlichen Vernunft' [On the Final Purpose of the Natural Dialectic of Human Reason] in *Werke*, VOL. 2 (Wilhelm Weischedel ed.). Frankfurt am Main: Insel Verlag, 1956, p. 588.

Page 73 ABOVE Kant, 'Grundsatz der Diätetik' [Principles of Dietetics] in *Werke*, VOL. 6, p. 376.

Page 73 BELOW Kant, 'Von der Hebung und Verhütung krankhafter Zufälle durch den Vorsatz im Atemziehen' [On the Improvement and Prevention of Sickness Through the Concentration on Drawing Breath] in *Werke*, VOL. 6, p. 386.

Page 74 ABOVE Kant, 'Erläuterung durch Beispiele' [An Explanation by Way of Examples] in *Werke*, VOL. 6, p. 552.

Page 74 BELOW Kant, 'Von der physischen Erziehung' [On Physical Education] in *Werke*, VOL. 6, p. 716.

Page 75 Kant, 'Grundsatz der Diätetik', p. 376.

Page 76 Kant, 'Von dem höchsten moralisch-physischen Gut' [Of the Highest Moral and Physical Good] in *Werke*, VOL. 6, p. 619.

LICHTENBERG'S WEEKLY PLANNER

Page 78 Georg Christoph Lichtenberg, *Sudelbücher* [Waste Books]. Wiesbaden: Marix Verlag, 2011, p. 94.

Page 79 Lichtenberg, *Sudelbücher*, p. 57.

Page 80 Georg Christoph Lichtenberg, *Aphorismen* [Aphorisms] (Kurt Batt ed.). Frankfurt am Main: Insel Verlag, 1976, p. 240.

Page 81 Lichtenberg, *Aphorismen*, p. 71.

Page 82 Lichtenberg, *Sudelbücher*, p. 55.

Page 83 Lichtenberg, *Aphorismen*, p. 128.

Page 84 Lichtenberg, *Sudelbücher*, p. 75.

AT AN ART EXHIBITION WITH HEGEL

Page 87 Georg Wilhelm Friedrich Hegel, *Vorlesungen über die Ästhetik I* [Lectures on Aesthetics I]. Frankfurt am Main: Suhrkamp Verlag, 1986, p. 214.

Page 88 ABOVE Hegel, *Vorlesungen*, p. 214.

Page 88 BELOW Hegel, *Vorlesungen*, p. 64.

Page 89 ABOVE Georg Wilhelm Friedrich Hegel, *Philosophie der Kunst*: *Vorlesung von 1826* [Philosophy of Art: Lecture of 1826] (Annemarie Gethmann-Siefert, Jeong-Im Kwon and Karsten Berr eds). Frankfurt am Main: Suhrkamp Verlag, 2004, p. 53.

Page 89 BELOW Hegel, *Vorlesungen*, p. 287.

Page 90 ABOVE Hegel, *Vorlesungen*, p. 65ff.

Page 90 BELOW Hegel, *Vorlesungen*, p. 66.

Page 91 ABOVE Hegel, *Vorlesungen*, p. 223.

Page 91 BELOW Hegel, *Vorlesungen*, p. 223

Page 92 Hegel, *Vorlesungen*, p. 224.

SCHOPENHAUER'S DRIVING SCHOOL

Page 95 Arthur Schopenhauer, 'Psychologische Bemerkungen, §305' [Psychological Observations, §305] in *Sämtliche Werkes, Band 5: Parerga und Paralipomena II* [Collected Works, Volume 5: Parerga and Paralipomena II] (Wolfgang Frhr. von Löhneysen ed.). Frankfurt am Main: Suhrkamp Verlag, 1986, p. 683.

Page 96 ABOVE Schopenhauer, 'Die beiden Grundprobleme der Ethik, §14: Antimoralische Triebfedern' [Two Fundamental Problems of Ethics, §14: Anti-Ethical Incentives] in *Sämtliche Werkes, Band 3*, p. 728.

Page 96 BELOW Arthur Schopenhauer, *Der handschriftliche Nachlaß, Band 1* [Manuscript Remains, Volume 1] (Arthur Hübscher ed.). Munich: dtv, 1985, p. 397.

Page 97 ABOVE Schopenhauer, 'Psychologische Bemerkungen, §324' [Psychological Observations, §324] in *Sämtliche Werkes, Band 5*, p. 694.

Page 97 BELOW Schopenhauer, 'Psychologische Bemerkungen, §324', p. 715.

Page 98 ABOVE Schopenhauer, 'Die Welt als Wille und Vorstellung, §57' [The World as Will and Representation, §57] in *Sämtliche Werkes, Band 1*, p. 431.

Page 98 BELOW Schopenhauer, 'Metaphysik der Geschlechtsliebe' [The Metaphysics of Sexual Love] in *Sämtliche Werkes, Band 2*, p. 697.

Page 99 ABOVE Schopenhauer, 'Die Welt als Wille und Vorstellung, §57', p. 16.

Page 99 BELOW Schopenhauer, 'Über Gelehrsamkeit und Gelehrte, §250' [On Scholarship and Scholars, §250] in *Sämtliche Werkes, Band 5*, p. 566. [*Ineptire est juris gentium*, that is, 'foolish is international law'.]

Page 100 Schopenhauer, 'Aphorismen zur Lebensweisheit: B. Unser Verhalten gegen uns selbst betreffend' [Aphorisms for the Wisdom of Life: B. Our Conduct in Regard to Ourselves] in *Sämtliche Werkes, Band 4*, p. 503.

DR KIERKEGAARD'S PRACTICE

Page 103 Søren Kierkegaard, 'Entweder–Oder' [Either–Or] in *Kierkegaard für Gestresste* [Kierkegaard for the Stressed-Out] (Johan de Mylius ed. and Ulrich Sonnenberg trans.). Frankfurt am Main: Insel Verlag, 2000, p. 49.

Page 104 ABOVE Kierkegaard, 'Abschließende unwissenschaftliche Nachschrift' [Concluding Unscientific Postscript] in *Kierkegaard für Gestresste*, p. 85

Page 104 BELOW Kierkegaard, 'Drei erbauliche Rede' [Three Edifying Discourses] in *Kierkegaard für Gestresste*, p. 36

Page 105 Kierkegaard, 'Die Wiederholung' [Repetition] in *Kierkegaard für Gestresste*, p. 33.

Page 106 Kierkegaard, 'Entweder–Oder, Diapsalmata' [Either–Or, Refrains], p. 32.

Page 107 ABOVE Kierkegaard, 'Erbauliche Reden in verschiedenem Geist' [Edifying Discourses in Diverse Spirits], p. 109.

Page 107 BELOW Kierkegaard, 'Entweder–Oder, Diapsalmata', p. 22.

Page 108 Kierkegaard, 'Entweder–Oder, Diapsalmata', p. 22.

IN THE SUPERMARKET WITH KARL MARX

Page 111 Karl Marx, *Ökonomisch-philosophische Manuskripte* [Economic and Philosophic Manuscripts]. Frankfurt am Main: Suhrkamp Verlag, 2009, p. 88.

Page 112 ABOVE Marx, *Ökonomisch-philosophische Manuskripte*, p. 88.

Page 112 BELOW Marx, *Ökonomisch-philosophische Manuskripte*, p. 90.

Page 113 Marx, *Ökonomisch-philosophische Manuskripte*, p. 90.

Page 114 ABOVE Marx, *Ökonomisch-philosophische Manuskripte,* p. 90.

Page 114 BELOW Marx, *Ökonomisch-philosophische Manuskripte*, p. 92ff.

Page 115 Marx, *Ökonomisch-philosophische Manuskripte*, p. 93.

CAMP FRIEDRICH NIETZSCHE

Page 119 Friedrich Nietzsche, *Menschliches, Allzumenschliches: Ein Buch für freie Geister* [Human, All Too Human: A Book for Free Spirits]. Frankfurt am Main: Insel Verlag, 1982, p. 274.

Page 120 ABOVE Nietzsche, *Menschliches, Allzumenschliches: Ein Buch für freie Geister*, p. 204

Page 120 BELOW Nietzsche, *Menschliches, Allzumenschliches: Ein Buch für freie Geister*, p. 278

Page 121 ABOVE Nietzsche, *Menschliches, Allzumenschliches: Ein Buch für freie Geister*, p. 412.

Page 121 BELOW Nietzsche, *Menschliches, Allzumenschliches: Ein Buch für freie Geister*, p. 354.

Page 122 ABOVE Nietzsche, *Menschliches, Allzumenschliches: Ein Buch für freie Geister*, p. 149.

Page 122 BELOW Friedrich Nietzsche, *Der Fall Wagner* [The Case of Wagner] (Dieter Borchmeyer ed.). Frankfurt am Main: Insel Verlag, 1983, p. 113

Page 123 ABOVE Friedrich Nietzsche, *Kritische Studienausgabe, Band 10: Nachgelassene Fragmente, 1882–1884* [Critical Edition, Volume 10: Unpublished Fragments] (Giorgio Colli and Mazzino Montinari eds). Munich: dtv/de Gruyter, 1980, p. 449.

Page 123 BELOW Friedrich Nietzsche, *Menschliches, Allzumenschliches: Band 2, Nachgelassene Fragmente, Fruehling 1878 bis November 1879* [Human, All Too Human, Volume 2: Unpublished Fragments, Spring 1878 to November 1879] (Giorgio Colli and Mazzino Montinari eds). Berlin: de Gruyter, 1967, p. 399.

Page 124 Nietzsche, *Menschliches, Allzumenschliches: Ein Buch für freie Geister*, p. 434.

BEDTIME STORIES WITH BERTRAND RUSSELL

Page 127 Bertrand Russell, 'Langeweile und Anregung' [Boredom and Stimulation] in *Eroberung des Glücks* [The Conquest of Happiness] (Magda Kahn trans.). Frankfurt am Main: Suhrkamp Verlag, 1977, p. 45.

Page 128 ABOVE Russell, 'Langeweile und Anregung', p. 45.

Page 128 BELOW Russell, 'Langeweile und Anregung', p. 42.

Page 129 Russell, 'Langeweile und Anregung', p. 42.

Page 130 ABOVE Russell, 'Langeweile und Anregung', p. 42.

Page 130 BELOW Russell, 'Langeweile und Anregung', p. 44

Page 132 Russell, 'Langeweile und Anregung', p. 46

WITTGENSTEIN'S BROOM SKETCH

Page 135 Ludwig Wittgenstein, *Philosophische Untersuchungen* [Philosophical Investigations] (Joachim Schulte ed.). Frankfurt am Main: Suhrkamp Verlag, 2003, p. 54.

Page 136 ABOVE Wittgenstein, *Philosophische Untersuchungen*, p. 54.

Page 136 BELOW Wittgenstein, *Philosophische Untersuchungen*, p. 53.

Page 137 Wittgenstein, *Philosophische Untersuchungen*, p. 54.

Page 138 ABOVE Wittgenstein, *Philosophische Untersuchungen*, p. 54.

Page 138 BELOW Wittgenstein, *Philosophische Untersuchungen*, p. 55.

Page 140 Wittgenstein, *Philosophische Untersuchungen*, p. 56.

A DREAM WEDDING WITH SIMONE DE BEAUVOIR

Pages 143–8 Simone de Beauvoir, *Das andere Geschlecht: Sitte und Sexus der Frau* [The Opposite Sex: The Morals and Sexuality of the Woman] (Uli Aumüller and Grete Osterwald trans). Reinbek bei Hamburg: Rowohlt Verlag, 1950, pp. 415–17.

BARTHES THE BEAR

Page 159 Roland Barthes, *Fragmente einer Sprache der Liebe* [Fragment of a Discourse on Love] (Hans-Horst Henschen trans.). Frankfurt am Main: Suhrkamp Verlag, 1988, p. 39.

Page 160 ABOVE Barthes, *Fragmente*, p. 39.

Page 160 BELOW Barthes, *Fragmente*, p. 44.

Pages 161–2 Barthes, *Fragmente*, p. 44.

Page 163 ABOVE Barthes, *Fragmente*, p. 48.

Page 163 BELOW Barthes, *Fragmente*, p. 99.

Page 164 Barthes, *Fragmente*, p. 243.

DELEUZE LEAVES THE CINEMA

Pages 167–70 Gilles Deleuze, *Das Bewegungs-Bild: Kino 1* [The Movement Image: Cinema 1] (Ulrich Christians and Ulrike Bokelmann trans). Frankfurt am Main: Suhrkamp Verlag, 1989, p. 279.

Page 171 Deleuze, *Das Bewegungs-Bild*, p. 281.

Page 172 Deleuze, *Das Bewegungs-Bild*, p. 223.

MICHEL FOUCAULT'S CABINET OF CURIOSITIES

Page 175 Michel Foucault, *Die Anormalen: Vorlesungen am Collège de France, 1974–1975* [The Abnormal: Annual Lectures at the Collège de France, 1974–1975] (Michaela Ott trans.). Frankfurt am Main: Suhrkamp Verlag, 2003, p. 380.

Page 176 Foucault, *Die Anormalen*, p. 383. [Charles Jouy, a forty-year-old nineteenth-century French farmhand, is represented here in accordance with Foucault's analysis, 'It must be shown that Charles Jouy and the little girl, whom he more or less violated, were ultimately close to each other, were of the same grain, of the same water . . .' See Foucault's lecture, 'Les anormaux: Cours du 19 mars 1975'. Available in French: https://bit.ly/2BEQ5fk (last accessed on 23 August 2018).]

Page 177 ABOVE Foucault, *Die Anormalen*, p. 80ff.

Page 177 BELOW Foucault, *Die Anormalen*, p. 85.

Page 178 Foucault, *Die Anormalen*, p. 85.

Pages 179–80 Foucault, *Die Anormalen,* p. 9.